USBORNE HOTSHOTS

FRIENDSHIP
BRACELETS

USBORNE HOTSHOTS

FRIENDSHIP
BRACELETS

Ray Gibson

Edited by Cheryl Evans and Anna Claybourne
Designed by Vicki Groombridge

Illustrated by John Woodcock
Photography by Howard Allman

Series editor: Judy Tatchell

CONTENTS

About friendship bracelets

Friendship bracelets make excellent presents for friends and relatives. The time you spend making one and choosing the design makes it a very personal gift.

What are they?

Friendship bracelets are knotted or plaited cotton bands which are given as a token of friendship - though you can make them for yourself too! You wear them tied around your wrist or ankle.

Where are they from?

Knotted, patterned friendship bracelets originally came from Central and South America. This book also contains some easy plaited versions.

What do they mean?

As well as being a sign of friendship, they are meant to bring good luck to the wearer. Make a wish when you are given one. It is supposed to come true when the bracelet finally wears out and falls off, but only if the bracelet has never been removed.

Make two bracelets the same - one for yourself and one for a friend - to signify the friendship between you.

Friendship bracelets can be all sorts of different sizes, shapes and thicknesses.

Some of the bracelets in this picture have beads added to them.

Choosing the thread

You can make friendship bracelets with any thick thread, but the best kind to use is six-stranded embroidery cotton. It comes in a huge variety of colours, and you can buy it in most department and craft stores.

You need quite a lot of thread for one bracelet. For a knotted bracelet, the threads need to be about 1m (3ft) long. However, some of the bracelets in this book use up less thread. Each pattern tells you how much you need.

Choose a mixture of dark and light threads to make your patterns show up best.

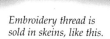

Embroidery thread is sold in skeins, like this.

Tools

The tools you will need are a good pair of scissors, some sticky tape and a safety pin.

Your scissors must be sharp so that they will trim ragged edges as neatly as possible. Sewing scissors are best.

Sticky tape is sometimes used instead of a pin.

Beads for decorating bracelets

Use a large, strong safety pin, like these.

5

Tips and techniques

Here are some basic techniques and methods to follow when you are making any of the friendship bracelets in this book. You can also use this page to refer back to for reminders and tips.

The patterned part of the bracelet fits around the wrist.

The width of the bracelet depends on how many threads you use.

The ends are used to tie it on.

What size?

Wrap a piece of string around your own or your friend's wrist, and cut it where it meets. Use this as a guide to show you how long the patterned part of the bracelet should be.

Knotting and pinning

While you are working on a bracelet, you need to hold it still. Do this by pinning it to an anchor point, such as your jeans, a cushion or an old chair.

HINT: If you are using a chair or sofa as an anchor point, make sure you ask the person who owns it first! The pin could pull at and damage some fabrics.

1. Begin by tying the threads together in a knot near one end. Remember to leave 10-15cm (4-6in) free for tying the bracelet on with.

2. Push the pin through the fabric, then through the knot in the threads, then through the fabric again. Close the pin.

3. Now you are ready to start on the bracelet. While you are working, pull the threads firmly away from the pin to keep the bracelet straight.

Finishing off

Most of the bracelets in this book need finishing off. When you have done the patterned part of a bracelet, tie a knot. Then plait together the loose threads at each end (see page 8 for how to plait). Finish each end with another knot, and trim the ragged ends.

Patterned part of bracelet

Handy tips

While you are knotting:
• Spread the threads out between steps, so they don't get tangled.
• Push knots up with your thumbnail and pull on the threads to keep them tight.
• Don't worry if it looks messy at first - the threads will soon sort themselves out.
• If you make a mistake, you can unpick knots with a pin or a sharp pencil.

Plait both ends of the bracelet until they are about 4cm (1.5in) long, or long enough to use to tie the bracelet onto your wrist.

Knot here.

Plaited part

Knot here.

Trim loose ends.

Using the diagrams

The diagrams for each stage show which thread is being moved. Look at the diagram before to check where it moved from. If you use different-coloured threads from those in the book, make a drawing before you start to remind you which is which.

Plaited bracelet

You can make a pretty bracelet very quickly this way. Choose three colours that blend together well, or a mixture of contrasting colours.

Plaiting

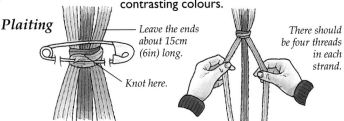

Leave the ends about 15cm (6in) long.

Knot here.

There should be four threads in each strand.

1. Cut four lengths of each of your three colours, about 40cm (15in) long. Knot and pin them together (see page 6).

2. Separate the threads into three strands, like this. Hold the two outer strands firmly, one in each hand.

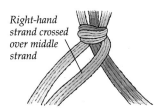

Right-hand strand crossed over middle strand

Left-hand strand crossed over middle strand

3. Start by crossing the right-hand strand over the middle strand. The right-hand strand will end up in the middle.

4. Now cross the left-hand strand over the new middle strand. Pull firmly on all the threads to keep them tight.

Tie a knot here.

Leave some thread at the end to tie the bracelet on with.

5. Keep plaiting in the same way, crossing first the right-hand strand, then the left-hand strand over the middle one.

6. Keep going until the bracelet is long enough to go around your wrist. Tie a knot at the end of the plait.

Tying the bracelet on

For this bracelet, don't plait the ends. Use them as they are to tie the bracelet on with.

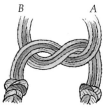

1. Cross A over B (left over right).

2. Tuck B through the loop.

3. Cross A over B (right over left).

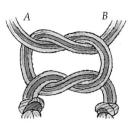

Trim the ends.

4. Tuck B through the loop.

5. Pull to tighten and trim off the ends.

You can add beads to a plaited bracelet (see page 17).

Try mixing lots of different colours together.

Plaiting patterns

Experiment with different shades to see how they look together.

This bracelet has a blend of pale pastel colours.

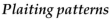

Beach bracelets

These summery bracelets are very quick to make, using a simple twisting method. You will need a selection of threads in natural shades, and a bead with a large hole.

Twisting method

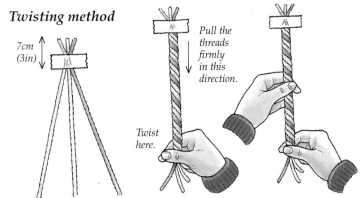

7cm (3in)

Pull the threads firmly in this direction.

Twist here.

1. Cut three threads about 60cm (24in) long. Tape them to a table top, leaving about 7cm (3in) free.

2. Hold the threads about 7cm (3in) from the other end. Pulling firmly, twist the threads tightly.

3. When the twist is very firm and tight, pinch it in the middle with your other hand.

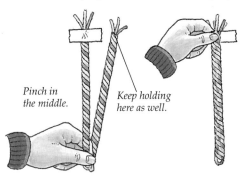

Pinch in the middle.

Keep holding here as well.

Looped end

4. Fold the twist in half so that the ends meet. Pull firmly to make sure both sides are even.

5. Now pull your thumb out of the loop. The bracelet will quickly twist around itself.

6. Take off the tape. Thread a bead onto the looped end of the bracelet. Push it up to the middle.

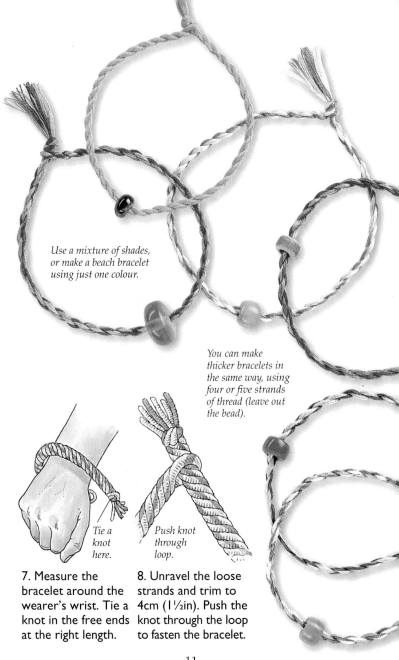

Use a mixture of shades, or make a beach bracelet using just one colour.

You can make thicker bracelets in the same way, using four or five strands of thread (leave out the bead).

Tie a knot here.

Push knot through loop.

7. Measure the bracelet around the wearer's wrist. Tie a knot in the free ends at the right length.

8. Unravel the loose strands and trim to 4cm (1½in). Push the knot through the loop to fasten the bracelet.

11

Four-way plaiting

This method uses four strands to make a smart, striped plait. It is a little more complicated than simple plaiting, but it's quick and easy once you get going.

Four-way striped bracelet

Follow the instructions closely and soon you'll be plaiting away without even needing to look at the pictures.

Each strand contains two threads.

The threads should now be in this order.

The strands look almost as they did to start with.

Four strands

1. Pick two colours and cut four 50cm (18in) pieces of each. Knot and pin them (see page 6) and arrange as shown.

2. To start plaiting, take the double strand on the far right. Pass it underneath the middle two strands.

3. Still holding the strand, bring it back over the last strand it passed under, so that it ends up looking like this.

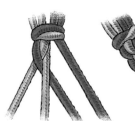

When the bracelet is long enough, tie a knot. Leave the ends long for tying on with.

4. Now do the same thing but from the other side. Take the left-hand strand, and pass it under the two middle strands.

5. Then bring it back over the nearest strand so that it ends up in between the two stands it has just passed under.

6. Keep repeating the pattern from step 2. Plait first from the right-hand side, then from the left-hand side.

12

Different styles

You can use the same method to make a range of different bracelets. Try these variations.

Make bracelets of different thicknesses by using three or four threads in each strand.

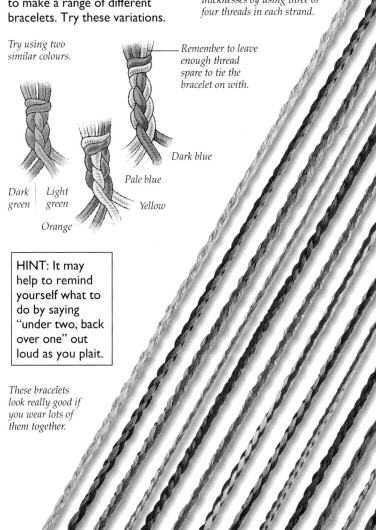

Try using two similar colours.

Remember to leave enough thread spare to tie the bracelet on with.

Dark blue

Pale blue

Yellow

Dark green   *Light green*

Orange

HINT: It may help to remind yourself what to do by saying "under two, back over one" out loud as you plait.

These bracelets look really good if you wear lots of them together.

Three-strand knotted bracelet

This is where you learn to do the knotting that is the basic technique for all traditional friendship bracelets. When you have practised the basic double knot, try the simple three-strand bracelet opposite.

How to knot

Each knot in a friendship bracelet is actually a double knot made up of two half-hitch knots. These pictures show you how to make one double knot.

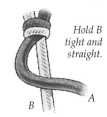

Hold B tight and straight.

B   A

1. Hold thread B taut in your left hand. Make a loop by crossing thread A over thread B.

A

B

2. Take the free end of thread A under thread B and up through the loop to make a loose knot.

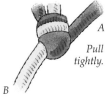

A

Pull tightly.

B

3. Slide the loop up to the top, then pull the thread with a sharp tug to tighten the knot.

A

B

4. Using the same two threads, knot thread A onto thread B again in exactly the same way.

Right-to-left knotting

The pictures above show left-to-right knotting. You can also knot in reverse by holding thread A and making a loop to the left with thread B. This is right-to-left knotting.

14

Three-strand bracelet

Cut three strands of thread 70cm (28in) long. Knot and pin them (see page 6). Knot each row from left to right as follows.

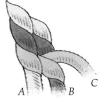

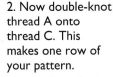

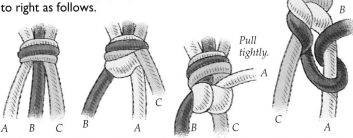

A B C

B

A

B C

C A

Pull tightly.

B

A

1. Using thread A, make a double knot, as described on the page opposite, onto thread B.

2. Now double-knot thread A onto thread C. This makes one row of your pattern.

3. Next, knot thread B onto thread C and then onto thread A. That makes the second row.

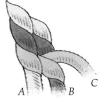

A B

C

Remember to do two knots each time.

4. Knot thread C onto thread A, then thread B. Now the threads are back where they started.

5. Keep repeating steps 1 to 4, always double-knotting the thread on the left onto the other two.

6. When the pattern is the right length, finish off the bracelet. (You will find help with this on page 7).

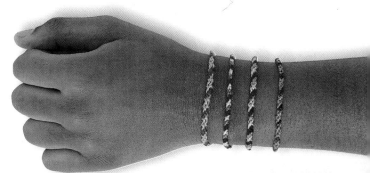

Striped and beaded bracelets

You can make wider striped bracelets in just the same way as the three-strand bracelet on page 15, but using four, six, or more threads. Remember to double-knot each thread in turn onto all the other threads. Look back to pages 14 and 15 if you get stuck.

To make stripy patterns

Try the arrangements below to get the patterns shown.

Lay out the threads in the pattern you want the stripes to appear. Two threads of the same colour together make a wide stripe made up of two rows of knots.

Start like this...

Start like this...

Each row of double knots makes one stripe in the pattern.

Start like this...

...for this pattern.

...for this pattern.

...for this pattern.

You could try some patterns of your own.

Add metallic beads to a bracelet for a bright effect (see right).

Narrow stripes

If you want narrow stripes, but a wide bracelet, use lots of threads arranged in a pattern like the one below. Each single thread makes a thin stripe made up of one row of knots.

Adding beads

You can buy beads from craft shops or special bead shops. Make sure the holes in the beads are big enough to take the thread you are using.

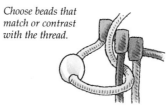

Choose beads that match or contrast with the thread.

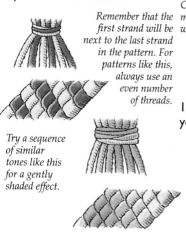

Remember that the first strand will be next to the last strand in the pattern. For patterns like this, always use an even number of threads.

Try a sequence of similar tones like this for a gently shaded effect.

1. Thread a bead onto the strand you are about to knot with.

Use the rows of stripes as a guide to help you space the beads evenly.

2. Now knot in the normal way. Knot to the end of the row and continue the pattern.

Try copying some of these patterns.

A rainbow pattern makes a beautiful bracelet.

Arrowhead bracelets

To make these patterns, you need to do left-to-right and right-to-left knotting (see page 14) in the same bracelet.

Making arrowhead bracelets

You will need four pairs of matching strands of thread, about 1m (3ft) long. Choose any colours you like.

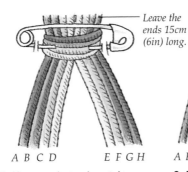

Leave the ends 15cm (6in) long.

A B C D   E F G H

1. Knot and pin the eight threads (see page 6). Arrange them in two equal groups of four, like this.

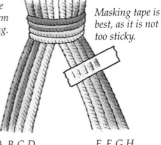

Masking tape is best, as it is not too sticky.

A B C D   E F G H

2. To make knotting easier, tape the second group off to one side while you work on the other side.

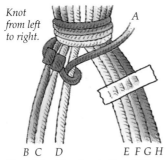

Knot from left to right.

A

B C D   E F G H

Thread A will end up in the middle.

3. Using thread A, make knots on B, C and D. Knot from left to right, just like making a simple bracelet.

B C D A   E F G H

4. Now tape threads B, C, D and A off to one side, keeping them in that order. Undo the tape on the other group.

18

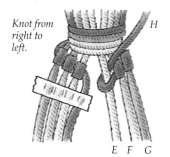

Knot from right to left.

H

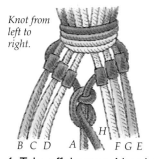

Knot from left to right.

E F G

B C D A H F G E

H

5. Now using right-to-left knotting (see page 14), knot thread H onto threads G, F and E. Work inwards from the right.

6. Take off the tape. Now knot thread A left-to-right onto thread H. This makes the point of the arrowhead.

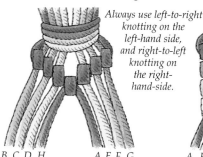

Always use left-to-right knotting on the left-hand side, and right-to-left knotting on the right-hand-side.

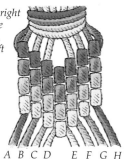

B C D H   A E F G

H and A have swapped places. This doesn't matter as they are the same colour.

A B C D   E F G H

Spread the threads out in order before starting again.

7. The arrowhead should look like this. Don't worry if it looks untidy at first - the threads will sort themselves out as you go.

8. Start again from step 2, always knotting from the outside into the middle. After the fourth time, it will look like this.

Keep working the pattern until the bracelet is long enough. After a while, you won't need to use the tape. See page 7 for how to finish the bracelet off.

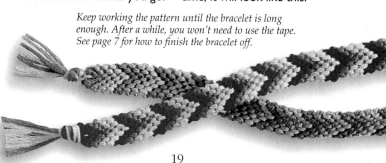

More arrowhead patterns

You can make different arrowhead patterns by changing the way the threads are laid out. Try these designs - or make up some new ones of your own.

Stripy arrowhead patterns

To make all these bracelets, use the arrowhead method shown on page 18. Before you start, lay the threads out in order. You can also add beads (see facing page).

Brightly contrasting colours work well in this pattern.

To make this pattern...

...start like this:

To make this pattern...

...start like this:

To make this pattern...

...start like this:

HINT: Every time you finish a row, spread the threads out in the right order before starting a new one.

This bracelet has beads added to it (see opposite).

20

For a shaded look

To get a shaded effect, choose a selection of similar colours, ranging from darker to lighter. Start with an arrangement of threads like this:

From a distance, the shaded pattern on the bracelet will look smoothly blended together.

Adding beads

Arrowhead bracelets look good with beads added to both sides. See page 17 for how to attach the beads.

You could arrange them like this.

Choose beads that make a pattern with the stripes in the bracelet.

Add beads to every row for a very decorative bracelet.

You could try making wider arrowhead bracelets with ten threads instead of eight.

Two strands of the same colour together make thicker arrowheads.

Star pattern

This pattern uses the arrowhead technique shown on page 18, but the arrowheads change direction in the middle of the bracelet, leaving a central star pattern.

Making a star pattern bracelet

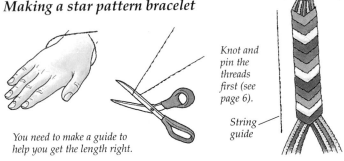

Knot and pin the threads first (see page 6).

String guide

You need to make a guide to help you get the length right.

1. Using a piece of string, measure the length around your friend's wrist and cut to this length. Then cut the string in half to make a guide.

2. Knot and pin threads for an arrowhead pattern (see page 18). Work the pattern as on pages 18-19, until it is about ½cm (¼in) shorter than the guide.

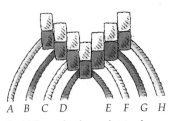

A B C D   E F G H

B   A C D   E F H G

3. When the bracelet is the right length, spread all the threads out evenly in the right order, before going on to the next stage.

4. Take thread A and knot it from left to right onto thread B. Then take thread H and knot it from right to left (see page 14) onto thread G.

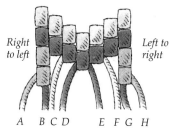

Right to left *Left to right*

A B C D E F G H

5. Now knot A back onto B, but this time from right to left. Knot H onto G from left to right. A and H should now be back at their starting places.

Right to left *Left to right*

D A B C F G H E

6. Now start in the middle and knot thread D onto threads C, B and A, knotting from right to left. Then knot E onto F, G and H, knotting from left to right.

Knot C onto F from left to right.

You are now doing the normal arrowhead pattern, but backwards.

Right to left *Left to right*

D A B F C G H E

7. You are now working in reverse. Make the point of the next arrowhead by knotting the two central threads C and F together, from left to right.

Right to left *Left to right*

F D A B G H E C

8. Knotting from right to left, knot F onto B, A and D. Then, knotting from left to right, knot C onto G, H and E. Then repeat the pattern from step 7.

Keep repeating the pattern, always starting by knotting the two central threads.

Keep going until the second half is as long as the first.

When the bracelet is long enough, plait and finish (see page 7).

Mermaids' beads

This is a slightly different kind of bracelet, with a spiral of knots that look like beads running down a long tubular shape. It looks amazing, but it's really easy to make.

Making mermaids' beads

You will need six threads in different colours and some strong sticky tape. Cut the threads about 80cm (32in) long.

1. Knot the threads together, leaving about 10cm (4in) free at the end.

2. Tape the threads above the knot very firmly to the edge of a clean, dry table.

3. Pull out one thread, and hold the other five together as if they were one.

4. Make a single left-to-right half-hitch knot (see page 14), looping the single thread around the other five. Pull the thread up tightly. A small knot will form.

5. Keep knotting in the same way. The knots will go in a spiral. When the bracelet gets too twisted, take off the tape and reposition the bracelet.

6. To change the colour, pull out another thread near the last knot you made. Put the old thread with the rest and start knotting with the new one.

24

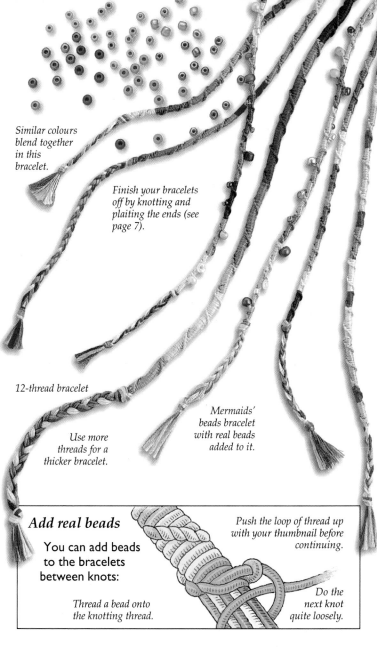

Similar colours
blend together
in this
bracelet.

Finish your bracelets
off by knotting and
plaiting the ends (see
page 7).

12-thread bracelet

Use more
threads for a
thicker bracelet.

Mermaids'
beads bracelet
with real beads
added to it.

Add real beads

You can add beads
to the bracelets
between knots:

Thread a bead onto
the knotting thread.

Push the loop of thread up
with your thumbnail before
continuing.

Do the
next knot
quite loosely.

Zigzag bracelets

This page shows you how to make a vibrant zigzag pattern. Use bright, glowing colours to make the pattern show up well.

Making a zigzag bracelet

The seventh thread will not show in the pattern.

A B C D E F G

1. Choose seven threads. Knot and pin them (see page 6).

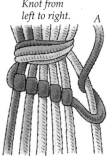

Knot from left to right.

A

B C D E F G
Row of six knots

2. Knot thread A left-to-right onto all the other threads.

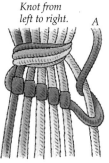

Do not knot B onto A.

B

A

C D E F G
Five knots

3. Knot B left-to-right to make a row of only five knots.

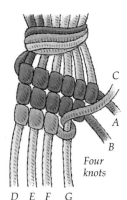

C

A

B

Four knots

D E F G

4. Knot C left-to-right to make a row of four knots.

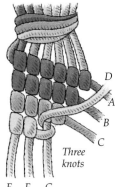

D

A

B

C

Three knots

E F G

5. Knot D left-to-right to make a row of three knots.

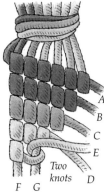

A

B

C

E

Two knots D

F G

6. Knot E left-to-right to make a row of only two knots.

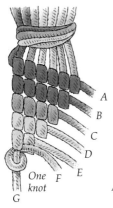

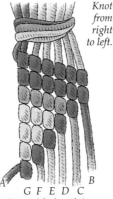

Knot
from
right
to left.

A
B
C
D
E
F
G

One knot

A   B
G F E D C
Start with thread A,
making a row of six knots.

B C D E F G
At the end, plait and finish
as usual (see page 7).

A

7. Knot F onto G from left to right, making one knot.

8. Now repeat from step 2, but knot right-to-left (see page 14).

9. Keep repeating the pattern. It will start to look like this.

More patterns to try

Try designing some different zigzag patterns by arranging your threads in different ways. These pictures may give you some ideas.

If A and B are the same colour, you will get a thick, chunky zigzag pattern.

Try "shadowing" the main zigzag by putting a darker shade next to it.

Always remember to pull the threads tightly towards you as you work.

Snake bracelets

This kind of bracelet has a wavy shape. For a snakeskin pattern, choose five shades ranging from dark to light.

Make a snake

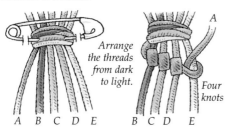

Arrange the threads from dark to light.

Four knots

Three knots

A   B   C   D   E

B   C   D   E

C   D   E   B

1. Choose five threads and knot and pin them (see page 6).

2. Knot thread A left-to-right on the other threads to make a row of four knots.

3. Knot B left-to-right onto C, D and E to make a row of three knots.

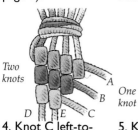

Two knots

D   E   C

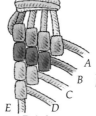

One knot

E   D

A
B
C

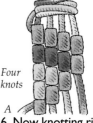

Four knots

A

4. Knot C left-to-right onto D and E to make a row of two knots.

5. Knot D left-to-right onto C to make a row of just one knot.

6. Now knotting right-to-left (see box), knot A onto all the other threads, B, C, D and E.

Hint

If you are unsure about right-to-left knotting, look at page 14 again. This picture may help.

Knot the right-hand thread around the thread to the left of it. Do this twice to make the double knot.

28

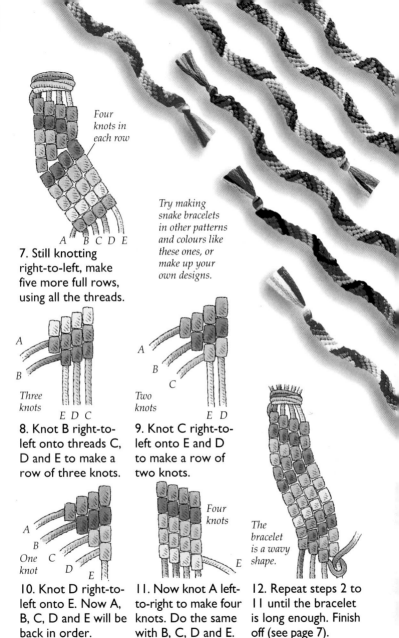

Four knots in each row

A B C D E

7. Still knotting right-to-left, make five more full rows, using all the threads.

Try making snake bracelets in other patterns and colours like these ones, or make up your own designs.

A

B

Three knots E D C

8. Knot B right-to-left onto threads C, D and E to make a row of three knots.

A

B

C

Two knots E D

9. Knot C right-to-left onto E and D to make a row of two knots.

A

B

One knot C

D E

10. Knot D right-to-left onto E. Now A, B, C, D and E will be back in order.

Four knots

E

11. Now knot A left-to-right to make four knots. Do the same with B, C, D and E.

The bracelet is a wavy shape.

12. Repeat steps 2 to 11 until the bracelet is long enough. Finish off (see page 7).

29

Criss-cross bracelet

This beautiful bracelet takes time to make, but it's worth the effort. It is made using left-to-right and right-to-left knotting in the same way as the arrowhead pattern on page 18.

Criss-cross method

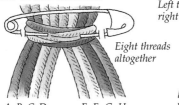

Eight threads altogether

Left to right

Right to left

A and H will end up in the middle.

A B C D   E F G H

B   C D A H E F   G

1. Choose four threads and cut two lengths of each. Knot and pin them (see page 6) in two equal groups, as shown here.

2. Knot thread A left-to-right onto threads B, C and D. Knot thread H right-to-left (see page 14) onto threads G, F and E.

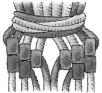

C D B A H G E F

D C B A H G F E

3. Knot B left-to-right onto C and D, making a row of two knots. Knot G right-to-left onto F and E in the same way.

4. Knot C left-to-right onto D, and knot F right-to-left onto E. You will have made two triangle shapes.

A and H will swap places.

H   *A*

D C B H A G F E

D   C   B G   F   E

5. Now take threads A and H, which are in the middle. Knot A left to right onto H to make a central knot.

6. Now start working outwards. Knot H right-to-left onto B, C and D. Knot A left-to-right onto G, F and E.